the
bench

Published by Barrington Stoke
An imprint of HarperCollins*Publishers*
Westerhill Road, Bishopbriggs, Glasgow, G64 2QT

www.barringtonstoke.co.uk

HarperCollins*Publishers*
Macken House, 39/40 Mayor Street Upper,
Dublin 1, DO1 C9W8, Ireland

This edition published in 2022

ISBN 978-1-80090-131-5

10 9 8 7 6 5 4 3

Printed by Ashford Colour

MIX
Paper | Supporting
responsible forestry
FSC™ C007454

This book contains FSC™ certified paper and other controlled
sources to ensure responsible forest management.

For more information visit: www.harpercollins.co.uk/green

the
bench

JO BROWNING WROE

Illustrated by
Kevin Hopgood

Barrington Stoke

An old man sits in the park. He is feeding the birds. It's cold. The icy wind cuts his face like a blade. A small boy stands on the path and looks at the man. He thinks the man's face looks kind.

"Hello," the boy says, and sits down next to the old man. The boy likes to chat.

"Good morning," says the man. He throws the last bit of bread to the birds and then he blows into his hands.

"Does that keep you warm?" asks

the boy.

"Not for long." The man smiles.
"How come you're on your own? Where
is your mum?"

"We're going to meet here," the boy

says. "She's always late. I'm used to it."

The old man feels sorry for the boy.

When his mum comes, he'll tell her it's bad

for a small child to be alone in the park.

"Have you ever seen a ghost?" asks the boy. He puts his hand softly on the man's arm.

"There's no such thing," the man says.

"How do you know?" the boy asks.

The old man shakes his head. "Humans like to be scared. Ghosts are a safe way to be scared."

"Is that what ghosts are for?" the boy asks. "To scare people?"

"Yes, in a way. Halloween and all that. It's a bit of fun. Why?"

"I'm trying to work out what ghosts are for. What they do," the boy tells him.

The man smiles. "You're a funny
little chap."

The Park Keeper comes to empty the bin next to the bench. "Hello," he says.

The old man nods his head, then turns back to the boy. "Where's that mum of yours?" he asks. "Do you think she'll be here soon?"

The Park Keeper leaves with his rubbish.

"What is it about that bench?" he says to himself. "It doesn't matter who sits on it, they always end up talking to the air."

He shakes his head and walks away.

HAVE YOU READ

the bench

JO BROWNING WROE

DATE WITH DANGER

JO BROWNING WROE

Ghost in the House

C.L.TOMPSETT

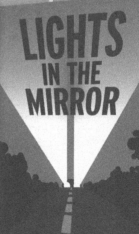

LIGHTS IN THE MIRROR

THEM <u>ALL</u>?

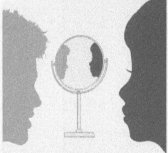